Fighting for CIVIL RIGHTS

Stephanie Loureiro

Contributing Author

Jenna Winterberg

Consultant

Jennifer M. Lopez, NBCT, M.S.Ed.
Teacher Specialist—History/Social Studies
Office of Curriculum & Instruction
Norfolk Public Schools

Publishing Credits

Rachelle Cracchiolo, M.S.Ed., *Publisher*
Conni Medina, M.A.Ed., *Managing Editor*
Emily R. Smith, M.A.Ed., *Content Director*
Véronique Bos, *Creative Director*
Robin Erickson, *Art Director*
Michelle Jovin, M.A., *Associate Editor*
Fabiola Sepulveda, *Graphic Designer*

Image Credits: front cover, p.1 Stephen F. Somerstein/Getty Images; pp.2–3, p.14 CSU Archives/Everett Collection/Newscom; p.4 Polaris/Newscom; p.5 (top) Everett Collection/Newscom; p.5 (bottom) Library of Congress [LC-USZ62-31799]; p.6 LOC [LC-DIG-fsa-8a26761]; p.7 (top) John McCutcheon; p.7 (bottom) LOC [LC-DIG-ppmsc-00199]; p.8, p.9 (left), p.11 (bottom), p.22 (bottom), p.23 (bottom) Bettmann/Getty Images; p.9 (right) LOC [LC-DIG-ds-11820]; p.10, p.15 U.S. National Archives; p.11 (top) Underwood Archives/Getty Images; p.12 John Duprey/NY Daily News Archive via Getty Images; p.13 (left) LOC [LC-USZ62-13035]; p.13 (right) The Print Collector/Heritage-Images/Newscom; p.16 World History Archive/Alamy; p.17 (top) Photo12/UIG/Getty Images; p.17 (bottom) Lee Balterman/The LIFE Picture Collection/Getty Images; p.18 LOC [LC-DIG-ds-10891]; p.19 (right) Ronald Reagan Presidential Library; p.19 (left) Kyodo News via Getty Images; p.20 Denver Post via Getty Image; p.21 (left) Arthur Schatz/The LIFE Picture Collection/Getty Images; p.21 (top right) Oregon State University Archives; p.22 (top) LOC [LC-DIG-hec-30741]; p.23 (top) Photo by SI Art Department /Sports Illustrated/Getty Images; p.24 Grey Villet/ The LIFE Premium Collection/Getty Images; p.25 (left) Cem Ozdel/Anadolu Agency/ Getty Images; p.25 (right) San José State University Special Collections & Archives; p.26 (left) Simon Davis/p.27 (top) arindambanerjee/Shutterstock; p.27 (bottom) Spiro Bolos/ Flickr; p.32 akg-images/Newscom; all other images from iStock and/or Shutterstock.

TCM Teacher Created Materials

5301 Oceanus Drive
Huntington Beach, CA 92649-1030
www.tcmpub.com
ISBN 978-1-4258-5078-4

Table of Contents

A Long Battle

People have been fighting for their rights for many years. Some people have fought for the right to vote. Other people have fought for the right to own property. Some people have even had to fight for the right to sit where they want on public buses. No matter what the reason may be, the fight for civil rights is an ongoing battle.

When people hear "civil rights," they likely think of the civil rights movement of the 1960s. That movement remains the most well-known example of a large group of people fighting for equality. However, there are many other groups of people who have done their own fighting. Government leaders have made bold moves for civil rights. Most battles, though, have actually taken place on the streets and in courtrooms. Many of these fights took place in the twentieth century. During that time, the **status quo** was tested. Progress was made toward social, legal, and economic justice. The ripple effect from this time can still be felt.

People fight for equality in 2019.

▲ Civil rights champion Rosa Park is arrested in 1955.

▲ Women fight for their right to vote.

Supremely Unfair

Congress passed a Civil Rights Act in 1875. It would have given all people certain rights. They would have had equal rights to housing, theaters, schools, cemeteries, and churches. But, the judges of the **Supreme Court** ruled the act was against the law. They said Congress could not control people's behaviors.

Types of Rights

There are two broad categories of rights. *Human rights* are rights that humans everywhere should have. *Civil rights* are rights that people have because they are citizens of a nation. These rights may change from country to country. People also have civil liberties. Some people use *civil rights* and *civil liberties* interchangeably, but there is a difference. Civil liberties protect people from government interference. Many of these can be found in the Bill of Rights. Civil rights are freedoms and can usually be found in **amendments**.

Fighting for Freedom

The History of Plessy

In 1892, Homer Plessy sat in the white section of a railcar. When Plessy refused to move to the black section of the train, he was arrested. Plessy appeared in court before Judge John H. Ferguson. Ferguson ruled that Plessy did not have a legal claim. The state supreme court agreed with Ferguson. This is why the case ended up before the U.S. Supreme Court.

Separate... But Not Equal

The Supreme Court ruled that segregation was legal. The court said black and white facilities could be separate but had to be equal in quality. This ruling came to be known as "separate but equal." The ruling was used to justify Jim Crow laws. Jim Crow laws were state and local laws that supported segregation. Many times, the facilities for black people were in much worse condition than those for white people.

In the nineteenth century, black people in the United States had few rights. In 1868, Congress passed the Fourteenth Amendment. It said all people born in the United States were citizens. Many white people did not like that black people now had the same rights as them. This law was designed to make sure that people of all races were treated as equals. However, that was not what happened. Black people were still treated very poorly in large parts of the country.

▲ A man drinks from a drinking fountain for black people in 1939.

▲ 1905 anti-Jim Crow laws cartoon

In 1896, *Plessy v. Ferguson* was brought before the Supreme Court. This legal case was about **segregated** railcars. The Plessy side argued segregation shouldn't be allowed. They said it went against the Fourteenth Amendment. The Ferguson side argued the law gave people citizenship but did not guarantee that everyone would be treated equally in society. The Supreme Court agreed with the Ferguson side. This ruling made segregation legal. After that, some states passed laws to keep black people and white people separated. Black people were forced to use different restrooms, parks, and even schools.

▲ This man waits in a black-only waiting room at a bus station in 1940.

Equal Education

Segregation lasted for decades. In 1950, a group of black parents wanted to enroll their students in a public school. However, they were refused because of their race. The parents fought back. The resulting case was *Brown v. Board of Education of Topeka, Kansas*. The case went all the way to the U.S. Supreme Court. This time, the judges agreed that segregation was wrong. So, in 1954, the Supreme Court ended "separate but equal." Black students could now attend formerly all-white schools.

Elizabeth Eckard, one of the Little Rock Nine, walks past a screaming crowd on her first day of school.

The **integration** of public schools was a big step forward. However, many schools in the South did not follow the law. In 1957, a group of nine black students arrived for their first day at Central High School in Little Rock, Arkansas. This was the first time black students would attend classes at the school. When the students got to the school, a crowd of white people threatened the students and threw stones at them. Members of the state's National Guard blocked the entrance. News of this attack spread across the world. The students tried to sneak into school but were seen and attacked. Twenty days later, the "Little Rock Nine" were **escorted** into school by U.S. soldiers and could finally attend classes.

▲ Thurgood Marshall with another civil rights leader and six of the Little Rock Nine outside the Supreme Court

Delayed Action

The Little Rock Nine had been chosen to attend Central High School for their excellent grades and attendance. President Dwight D. Eisenhower had to step in to keep them safe. He forced the state's National Guard to stop blocking the students' entry and start protecting them. Black students in other states were facing **discrimination** too. It took decades for full integration to occur.

Paving the Way

Thurgood Marshall was a lawyer. He represented the parents in *Brown v. Board of Education*. He argued that segregation in public schools was **unconstitutional**. After he won his case, Marshall went on to become the first black U.S. Supreme Court justice. From 1967 to 1991, Marshall served on the court. In that time, he worked to protect people's civil rights.

Freedom Riders

In 1946, the Supreme Court ruled that buses on **interstate** routes could not be segregated, but **intrastate** buses could be. So, in 1955, Martin Luther King Jr. led a bus **boycott**. He and his group refused to ride buses in Montgomery, Alabama. They thought the boycott would pressure the state to change its laws. The boycott lasted for more than a year. Then, the U.S. Supreme Court ruled that segregated buses everywhere were illegal. Four years later, the court went a step further. Bus stops, restrooms, and other services that were part of bus travel could no longer be segregated either.

On May 4, 1961, a group of black and white people tested the court's ruling by boarding two buses in Washington, DC. They were headed south to New Orleans. These people were part of a large group called the Freedom Riders. When the buses stopped along the route, white Freedom Riders used the facilities meant for black people and **vice versa**.

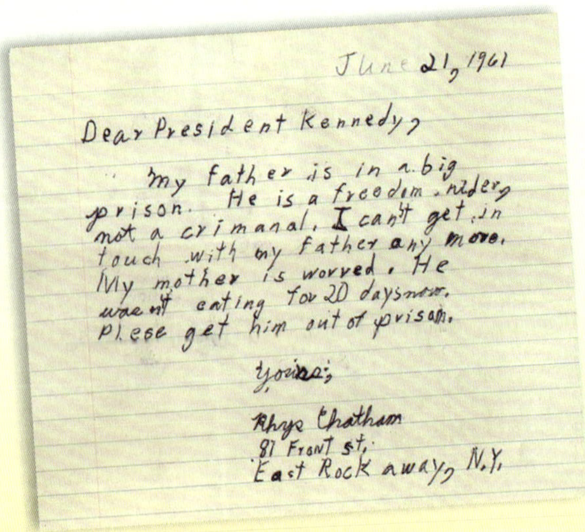

June 21, 1961

Dear President Kennedy,

My father is in a big prison. He is a freedom rider, not a crimanal. I can't get in touch with my father any more. My mother is worred. He was n't eating for 20 days now. Plese get him out of prison.

Yours,

Rhys Chatham
81 Front st,
East Rockaway, N.Y.

▲ A Freedom Rider's son asks President Kennedy to release his father from jail.

Before Parks

When Rosa Parks refused to give up her bus seat to a white man in 1955, she was arrested and the Montgomery bus boycott began. Parks became famous for her refusal. However, there were other women who protested before her. Aurelia Browder, Mary Louise Smith, Claudette Colvin, and Susie McDonald were mistreated on city buses. Their case, *Browder v. Gayle*, made it to the U.S. Supreme Court. It was their case that made all bus segregation illegal.

Another Way

On February 1, 1960, four black college students sat at the white-only lunch counter at a Woolworth's general store in Greensboro, North Carolina. People yelled at them and poured drinks on their heads. However, they sat through it all and came back the next day. More students joined them. TV news stations reported on the **sit-ins**. Within a month, people in 13 states had staged their own sit-ins. The Woolworth's counter was integrated by July.

Things became very violent when the riders were in Alabama. One of the bus drivers stopped to fix a flat tire. While the bus was stopped, someone **firebombed** it. The Freedom Riders rushed off the bus. An angry crowd beat the riders with baseball bats as they left the bus. In spite of this, more people followed their lead. Some Freedom Riders were arrested. President John F. Kennedy supported them. He said that all people should be safe to ride buses.

▼ Freedom Riders gather outside their firebombed bus on May 14, 1961.

▲ Freedom Riders leave New York City for Washington, DC, on May 30, 1961.

Campaigning for Change

In April 1963, King took charge once more. He led a series of nonviolent sit-ins, boycotts, and marches. These events were known as the Birmingham Campaign. At one of the marches, King was arrested. When he was in jail, he wrote the now-famous "Letter from Birmingham Jail." In it, King argued that the right to peacefully protest belonged to all Americans.

King's actions and letter inspired people. A few weeks later, more than one thousand teenagers led a peaceful protest. They were called the Birmingham Children's Crusade. White police officers attacked the teens and beat them with **batons**. They set attack dogs on them. Firefighters sprayed the teens with fire hoses. All these events were shown on national TV. People were horrified by what they saw.

▼ Members of the Birmingham Children's Crusade are sprayed with high-power fire hoses.

In June, President Kennedy proposed a new civil rights act that would make all segregation illegal. Days later, civil rights leaders told Kennedy that they were planning a national demonstration. Kennedy thought a big demonstration might hurt his chances of getting his act passed. However, the leaders said they had to take action. So, Kennedy secretly allowed members of his staff to help with the protest.

▲ President Kennedy

Why Birmingham?

Racism and segregation took place in many areas of the country. However, it was most common in the South. Birmingham, Alabama, was one of the most segregated cities in the country. Racist acts were frequent there. Between 1947 and 1966, there were around 50 bombings of black churches and homes in Birmingham.

Inspiring Nonviolence

Mohandas Gandhi was an Indian civil rights leader. He believed peaceful protests were the best way to win support for a cause. Gandhi began his protests after he was removed from a train for refusing to move out of the first-class section, even though he held a first-class ticket. King wrote that Gandhi was "the guiding light" behind his own nonviolent protests.

Turning Point

On August 28, 1963, more than 250,000 people gathered in front of the Lincoln Memorial. This became known as the March on Washington for Jobs and Freedom. While there, King gave his "I Have a Dream" speech. King's moving speech and the massive march helped open many Americans' eyes. People from all over the country were tired of the way African American people were being abused. The march sparked a turning point.

Kennedy planned to move his new act forward. Sadly, just three months later, Kennedy was **assassinated**. As Americans grieved the loss of their leader, the civil rights movement paused. No one was sure what the new president—Lyndon B. Johnson—would do next.

King (front row, sixth from right) and other civil rights champions lead the March on Washington.

Johnson promised to continue Kennedy's work. He signed the Civil Rights Act of 1964 into law. The act made it illegal to discriminate against a person based on their race, **nationality**, religion, or gender. Next, the Voting Rights Act and the Twenty-Fourth Amendment passed. These two laws made it illegal to charge voters taxes or to require tests before someone can vote. Before then, many states charged poll taxes, which were fees that people had to pay when they registered to vote. Literacy tests were meant to prove that voters could read and write. The signing of these laws brought an end to Jim Crow laws.

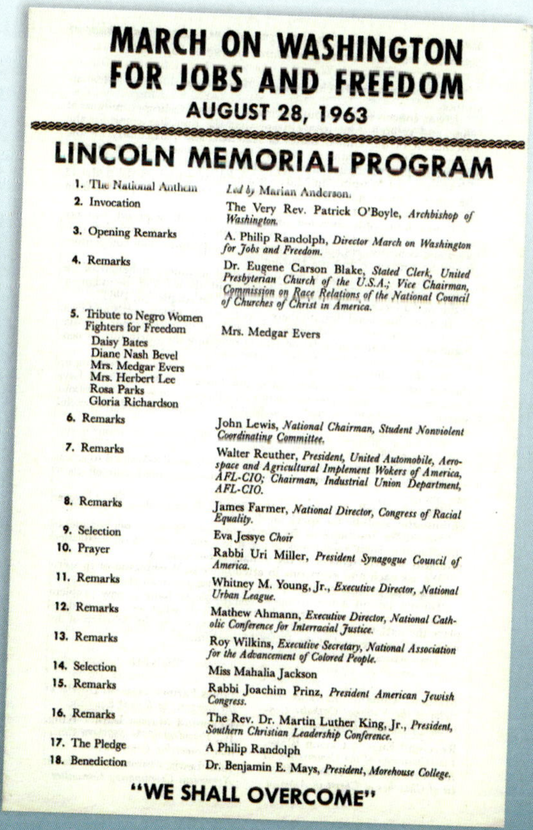
MARCH ON WASHINGTON FOR JOBS AND FREEDOM
AUGUST 28, 1963

LINCOLN MEMORIAL PROGRAM

1. The National Anthem	*Led by* Marian Anderson.
2. Invocation	The Very Rev. Patrick O'Boyle, *Archbishop of Washington.*
3. Opening Remarks	A. Philip Randolph, *Director March on Washington for Jobs and Freedom.*
4. Remarks	Dr. Eugene Carson Blake, *Stated Clerk, United Presbyterian Church of the U.S.A.; Vice Chairman, Commission on Race Relations of the National Council of Churches of Christ in America.*
5. Tribute to Negro Women Fighters for Freedom Daisy Bates Diane Nash Bevel Mrs. Medgar Evers Mrs. Herbert Lee Rosa Parks Gloria Richardson	Mrs. Medgar Evers
6. Remarks	John Lewis, *National Chairman, Student Nonviolent Coordinating Committee.*
7. Remarks	Walter Reuther, *President, United Automobile, Aerospace and Agricultural Implement Wokers of America, AFL-CIO; Chairman, Industrial Union Department, AFL-CIO.*
8. Remarks	James Farmer, *National Director, Congress of Racial Equality.*
9. Selection	Eva Jessye *Choir*
10. Prayer	Rabbi Uri Miller, *President Synagogue Council of America.*
11. Remarks	Whitney M. Young, Jr., *Executive Director, National Urban League.*
12. Remarks	Mathew Ahmann, *Executive Director, National Catholic Conference for Interracial Justice.*
13. Remarks	Roy Wilkins, *Executive Secretary, National Association for the Advancement of Colored People.*
14. Selection	Miss Mahalia Jackson
15. Remarks	Rabbi Joachim Prinz, *President American Jewish Congress.*
16. Remarks	The Rev. Dr. Martin Luther King, Jr., *President, Southern Christian Leadership Conference.*
17. The Pledge	A Philip Randolph
18. Benediction	Dr. Benjamin E. Mays, *President, Morehouse College.*

"WE SHALL OVERCOME"

▶ official schedule for the March on Washington

Sample Literacy Test

Test officials chose what to ask in literacy tests. They could use that power to discriminate. A white voter might have to name the president. A black voter might have to answer trickier questions. One question from the 1960 Louisiana literacy test was "Spell *backwards* forwards." (The answer was *b-a-c-k-w-a-r-d-s*.) Another question was "What is the last letter of the first word beginning with 'L'?" (The answer was *T*, since *last* was the first word beginning with "L.")

Killing Kennedy

On November 22, 1963, President Kennedy was shot while he rode in the back of a car. Texas Governor John Connally was also shot. Both men were rushed to a nearby hospital. Connally survived, but Kennedy did not. Lee Harvey Oswald was arrested for the shooting. Two days later, a man named Jack Ruby shot and killed Oswald on live TV. Kennedy's death and the events after rocked the nation.

A New Age

By the mid-1960s, the civil rights movement was in full force. King argued for nonviolent protests. However, not everyone felt the same way. As the years stretched on, some people felt that if their rights were at risk, they had a duty to fight back.

In October 1966, some civil rights **activists** formed the Black Panther Party. The group's goal was to make sure that civil rights laws were being followed. The Black Panthers wanted to defend and improve their communities. They set up health clinics, food drives, and centers for legal help. As time went on, though, government officials began blaming the Black Panther Party for an increase in violence. Tensions between the Black Panthers and the government rose.

On April 4, 1968, King was standing on a hotel balcony in Memphis, Tennessee. Suddenly, King crumpled to the ground. He had been shot in the neck. King was rushed to a hospital, where he was pronounced dead. The assassination of the country's most notable civil rights activist had a huge impact. King had always believed in nonviolent actions, yet violence had taken him away. People in over a hundred cities **rioted** in response to his death.

Cost of Rioting

Between 1964 and 1971, there were more than 750 riots across the country. One of the most damaging riots took place in Watts, California, in 1965. The Watts Riot lasted from August 11 to August 16. In that time, 35 people died. Almost one thousand buildings were destroyed. There was more than $40 million in damage done. (That is about $320 million in today's money.)

Robert's Remarks

On April 4, John Kennedy's younger brother, Robert, was in Indiana campaigning for the presidency. Instead of his prepared speech, he stunned the crowd with news of King's death. Robert acknowledged that some people might be "tempted to be filled with hatred and distrust at the injustice." He asked instead that the crowd join him in forming a more peaceful future. Sadly, Robert Kennedy would not live to see that future. Only 68 days after King's death, Robert was also assassinated.

Members of the Black Panther Party march in the 1960s.

Americans riot after King's murder.

Fighting for Equality

The civil rights movement focused mostly on equal rights for African American people. However, there were other groups who were fighting for their rights as well.

Japanese Americans

In 1941, Japanese pilots attacked a U.S. naval base in Hawai'i. After that, some people thought Japanese Americans were **traitors**. People thought they would attack the United States. So, President Franklin D. Roosevelt signed a law. It forced all Japanese people and Japanese Americans living on the West Coast to move. They were sent to live in **internment camps**. They had to leave their friends, businesses, and homes behind.

▼ Internees wave goodbye to people who are leaving the camp.

Around 120,000 people were forced to live in internment camps. Two-thirds of them had been born in the United States. People around the country protested this act. In 1944, the issue was brought before the U.S. Supreme Court. A man named Fred Korematsu had refused to move to the camps and had been arrested for his refusal. In front of the court, his side argued that his rights as a U.S. citizen should keep him safe from discrimination. The court ruled against Korematsu. It said that "the power to protect" was the most important.

The court's decision made the camps legal. However, more and more Americans were speaking out against them. The government eventually gave in to public pressure. The last of the camps closed in March 1946.

An Apology

After World War II ended, people who lived in the camps were freed. They asked lawmakers to apologize for the camps. For many years, they did not get what they wanted. Then, President Ronald Reagan signed the Civil Liberties Act of 1988. The act gave tens of thousands of camp survivors $20,000 each. The government also officially apologized to each person who had lived in the camps.

A man who was born in an internment camp shows his letter of apology from the U.S. government.

The Case

Not all U.S. Supreme Court justices agree with every ruling. In *Korematsu v. United States*, six judges voted to keep the camps. Three judges voted against the camps. Those three judges wrote a statement about why they disagreed. They wrote that Korematsu was being punished for being in the wrong place at the wrong time.

Workers' Rights

Before World War II, many Japanese Americans were farmers. In fact, in the city of El Monte, California, Japanese Americans owned around four-fifths of all berry fields. When they were sent to internment camps, a lot of farms were left unattended. Government leaders knew they had to keep these farms running. So, they asked farmers to come from Mexico. Millions of people answered the call and found work. However, in many jobs, the working conditions were poor. The pay was often low, and the work could be very dangerous.

A man named Cesar Chavez saw these struggles. He was born to immigrants who worked on farms. He wanted to help workers. So, he turned to another person he knew who was fighting for rights. Her name was Dolores Huerta. Chavez and Huerta formed a **union** for all farm workers. The group organized marches and boycotts.

In 1965, Filipino American workers called for a boycott on grape growers. They wanted better working conditions and more pay. The boycott lasted for years. Eventually, with help from the farm workers union, farmers forced grape field owners to meet their demands. The workers were able to get better pay, working conditions, and healthcare.

Grape farmers protest unfair working conditions.

Huerta and Chavez discuss the grape growers protest in 1968.

Braceros

When World War II began, farms suffered. Many farm owners and workers had either been sent to internment camps or were fighting overseas. So, the U.S. government asked Mexican workers to work as part of the Bracero Program. The program began in 1942. Workers signed contracts, which let them work short-term jobs in the United States. The program ended in 1964. By then, 4.7 million people had found work through the Bracero Program.

Working Together

Huerta and Chavez first met in the 1950s. Before that, Huerta had been fighting for rights for noncitizens working in the United States. When she met Chavez, he inspired her to help farmers. In 1962, Chavez and Huerta formed a union. It was called the National Farm Workers Association. It was later renamed the United Farm Workers of America. The union is still around and has helped millions of farm workers.

Women's Rights

In 1848, Elizabeth Cady Stanton and Lucretia Mott organized the Seneca Falls Convention. The meeting was held to discuss women's right to vote and the fight for equality. With this meeting, the women's rights movement had begun.

Three years later, Stanton met another leader named Susan B. Anthony. The two women made a strong team. They worked together to get women the right to vote. Stanton and Anthony dedicated their lives to this cause. Their goal would be reached decades later in 1920. That is when the Nineteenth Amendment became law. It gave American women the legal right to vote. Sadly, Stanton and Anthony had both died before this happened.

▲ Women protest outside the White House in 1917.

Voting Rights

The fight for women's **suffrage** gained momentum during World War I. Women entered the workforce and felt they had earned their right to vote. In 1917, a group of feminists protested outside the White House. Several of them were arrested. President Woodrow Wilson was horrified when he heard about how they were being treated in jail. After that, Wilson spoke to Congress of his support for women's suffrage and persuaded them to approve the amendment.

Women's March

The second wave of feminism ended in the 1980s. It was followed by third- and fourth-wave feminism. Fourth-wave feminists want everyone to feel safe and heard in society. One way they do this is by marching. On January 21, 2017, people all over the world joined the first Women's March. In the United States, almost five million people marched, making it the largest single-day demonstration in U.S. history.

Title IX

What It Does

Title IX makes sure that school programs don't discriminate against people based on gender. It applies to all schools (both public and private) that receive federal funding.

What It Means

Men and women must be given equal opportunities in school programs, sports, and activities. They must have similar equipment, supplies, and facilities.

What It Does Not Mean

Title IX does not mean all programs have to be the same. Differences between male and female programs are allowed, as long as they are reasonable and not based on discrimination.

How It Works

Schools are responsible for following Title IX requirements. If they do not, the U.S. Department of Education can fine schools or even take away their government funding.

The right to vote is usually seen as the end of the period known as "first-wave **feminism**." The next years saw the Great Depression and World War II. Women's rights were put on hold while the nation was in crisis. Then, in the 1960s, second-wave feminism began. During this time, women fought for equal rights in jobs and schools. In the 1970s, they saw some key wins. Laws were passed that said school sports teams and programs could not discriminate against people based on gender. These laws are called Title IX. They are still in effect.

▼ Boston Marathon runners stop an official from removing Kathrine Switzer (261) from the race in 1967. Five years later, women were allowed to enter the race.

LGBTQ Rights

The LGBTQ community includes many people. It is made up of groups of people who have similar gender identities and sexual orientations. For many years, these people have faced discrimination.

The first major fight for LGBTQ rights took place in 1969. New York City police officers heard that a popular gay bar—the Stonewall Inn—was selling alcohol without a license. Officers searched the bar and arrested people inside. As they hauled people out of the bar, the officers handled them roughly. Other people in the bar spoke out against the abuse. More people from the neighborhood saw the rough treatment and joined in. For the next six days, hundreds of people rioted.

▶ LGBTQ rights activists fight for equal employment rights in 1971.

The Stonewall Riots did not start the gay rights movement. However, they did urge people to take action. LGBTQ rights groups, such as the Human Rights Campaign and GLAAD, formed at this time. These groups are still around.

Over time, the LGBTQ community has become more widely accepted. In 2015, the Supreme Court ruled that same-sex marriage was legal. Now, all people had the right to get married.

▼ **LGBTQ rights activists celebrate the legalization of same-sex marriage in 2015.**

What Does LGBTQ Mean?

The letters stand for *lesbian*, *gay*, *bisexual*, *transgender*, and *queer* or *questioning*. The number of people who identify as LGBTQ is growing. **Demographers** shared a recent survey. They found that 1 in 25 people in the United States identifies as LGBTQ. Demographers predict this number may continue to grow.

Milk's Impact

In 1977, Harvey Milk became one of the first openly gay politicians. Sadly, one year later, Milk was assassinated. Milk's death affected many people. It caused more LGBTQ people to enter politics.

The Fight Continues

Civil rights are unique types of rights. Unlike human rights—which people earn simply by being born—civil rights have to be granted. That is why it is important for people to fight for their rights. Change can and does happen, even when it takes a long time.

The United States has a long history of people fighting for their rights. In fact, the country was founded on the right to representation. In the years since, there has been a great deal of progress for civil rights. However, there is still a long way to go.

A Movement

Recent years have played host to many civil rights and civil liberties demonstrations. Movements such as Occupy Wall Street, Me Too, Black Lives Matter, Time's Up, and March for Our Lives have large followings. They have caused many people to look closely at how others are treated.

A Global Fight

It is not just Americans who are fighting for their rights. Malala Yousafzai was born in Pakistan. A group called the Taliban banned Pakistani girls and women from getting an education. She did not agree with this and went to school anyway. The Taliban reacted by shooting her in the head three times. Incredibly, she survived. Yousafzai went back to school. She now works to help other people fight for their rights.

▲ Children have the power to change the future.

Officially, the U.S. civil rights movement lasted through the 1960s. However, many Americans still stand up for equality. Recent civil rights movements have proven that there is work to be done. They have also shown that people are willing to put in the work. Luckily, they are not starting from nothing. Rather, they are continuing the legacy that came before them. They are becoming part of the long history of fighting for civil rights.

▲ **Hundreds of thousands of people participated in the 2018 civil liberties demonstration—March for Our Lives.**

Design It!

Many activists today use social media to get their messages across. For example, to bring attention to the use of police force, activists created the hashtag #BlackLivesMatter. People use the hashtag to share their thoughts and pictures on social media. Famous actors and athletes are among those people who have used social media to show their support for recent campaigns.

Choose a civil rights cause that's important to you. It may be something you read about in this book or something else you feel passionate about. Design a social media campaign for the cause. Will you spread your message with hashtags? Will you create a symbol for your movement? Will you encourage other people to share their stories? Which social media platform will best fit your campaign's goals? It's up to you! Think about the best way to gain support for your cause and the response you think your campaign would get.

Glossary

activists—people who believe in mass demonstrations for political purposes

amendments—changes to the words or meanings of laws or documents

assassinated—killed

batons—clubs or sticks that are carried by many law enforcement officers

boycott—a refusal to work with a country, organization, or person to express disapproval and to force them to accept terms

demographers—people who study human populations

discrimination—unfair treatment of a person or group

escorted—accompanied by a person or group for protection

feminism—the theory that supports equality of the sexes

firebombed—attacked something with a bomb that causes a fire to ignite

integration—the process of joining people from different races

internment camps—prisons where people are kept for political reasons during wars

interstate—occurring between two or more states

intrastate—occurring within one stat

nationality—the country a person comes from

rioted—behaved in a way that caused public disturbance

segregated—separated by race, religion, or other factors

sit-ins—a form of protest that involve occupying spaces and refusing to lea

status quo—the existing state of affai

suffrage—the right to vote

Supreme Court—the highest court of the United States

traitors—people who betray others

unconstitutional—not agreeing with or according to the constitution of a society or country

union—a group of workers formed to protect the interests and rights of its members

vice versa—a Latin phrase meaning that the reverse of a phrase is also tr

Index

Your Turn!

This photograph shows people at the March on Washington for Jobs and Freedom. This march was one of the largest civil rights rallies in U.S. history. A crowd of around 250,000 people listened to speeches from 10 activists and community leaders. The most famous speech from the day was Martin Luther King Jr.'s "I Have a Dream" speech.

Read some or all of King's speech from that day. What makes it so powerful? How did King urge the crowd to both remember the past and look forward to the future?

Imagine you have been asked to speak to a crowd about a civil rights issue you are passionate about. Write your own speech using what you have learned from King's speech. Then, deliver your speech to friends or family members. Remember to speak about your topic with passion and energy.